Mac's Christmas Star

Margaret Forrester and Sandra Klaassen

For Mairi – M.F.

For my mum and auntie – S.K.

Picture Kelpies is an imprint of Floris Books. First published in 2012 by Floris Books. Text © 2012 Margaret Forrester.
Illustrations © 2012 Sandra Klaassen. Margaret Forrester and Sandra Klaassen assert their right under the Copyright,
Designs and Patents Act 1988 to be identified as the Author and Illustrator of this Work. All rights reserved.
No part of this publication may be reproduced without the prior permisson of
Floris Books, 15 Harrison Gardens, Edinburgh, EH11 1SH www.florisbooks.co.uk
The publisher acknowledges subsidy from Creative Scotland towards the publication of this volume.
British Library CIP Data available. ISBN 978-086315-842-1. Printed in China.

Mac lives in a tall, thin house in Edinburgh. It is his house.
He has lived in it for a long time.

A family lives in Mac's house.
There are four people in the
family:
  a mum,
  a dad,
  a boy called Donald

and a girl called Catriona,
who is Mac's special friend.

On Christmas Eve, everyone was busy.

Dad asked, "Who wants to come and pick up our Christmas tree?"

"I do!" Donald and Catriona shouted.

"Wrap up well," warned Mum.
"It's bitterly cold."

"I'll get my gloves," said Catriona, and she rushed upstairs. Mac followed.

"Not in there, Mac," called Catriona. "We aren't allowed in Mum and Dad's room. Secrets."

Mac was on Mum and Dad's bed, his tail curled round a pretty box.

"I wonder if that's for me?" Catriona opened the box.

A necklace of glittering stars lay there, with a bracelet
and ring to match.
  "Oh!" she whispered,
and she tried on the ring.

  "What're you doing?" Donald put his head round the door.
  "Nothing," said Catriona. She snapped the box shut, pulled
on her gloves and clattered downstairs.

They returned home an hour later with an enormous
Christmas tree fastened to the car.

"Oh my!" said Mum. "The biggest tree in the forest!"
"What a lovely tree for me to climb," purred Mac.

Mum held onto the pointy bit at the top of the tree and tried to guide it into the sitting room. But it wouldn't go round the corner.

"We could push it through the window," said Donald.
"Good idea!" said everyone.

Dad and Donald pushed from outside.
One, two, three, PUSH!

Mum and Catriona pulled from inside.
One, two, three, PULL!

Finally the tree was
standing upright.

Mac stared at it. It
smelt of forest, fresh
air and fir cones.

"Well done!" said Mum. "Time for
lunch. Wash hands, everyone."
It was then that Catriona remembered
about the ring. But it wasn't there!

While everyone was tucking into soup and mince pies, Mac decided to investigate the tree.

At the top there was a tiny sparkle. "Maybe that's a star," he thought.

Cautiously he started to climb. The tree began to sway and wobble...

The door opened.
"Mac, no!" yelled Donald.
"Mac, come down!" called Catriona.
"Get that cat out of here!" shouted Dad.

"We'll have to put Mac out while
we decorate the tree," decided Mum.
So Mac was banished.

While Dad and Donald sorted out the fairy lights, Catriona looked for the ring, and Mac helped her.

They looked on the front path...

on the pavement...

... and beside the window that the tree had gone through.
"Get down, Mac," whispered Catriona. "They'll see us."
"What are you doing, Catriona?" called Dad. "Come in
and help decorate the tree."

Dad turned on the fairy lights. "That's done," he said, admiring his handiwork. "Now you can decorate the rest of the tree."

Altogether they had:

1 shepherd's crook

2 apples

3 lambs

4 reindeer

5 robins

6 doves

7 candles

8 snowflakes

9 bells

10 angels

dozens of baubles

and lots and lots and lots of tinsel.

"It's lovely," said Catriona, as she tied on the last angel.

"Wow," said Mum, "you've worked really hard."

"That," said Dad, blinking, "is a Much Decorated Tree."

Mac slipped in when no one was looking. Underneath all the tinsel, he could still see his star.

"I really want that star," he thought.

Dad went to do his Christmas shopping. Donald went to play with a friend. Mum went upstairs to wrap presents.

Catriona cuddled Mac. "We must find that ring. Please help me. This is not how Christmas is supposed to be."

They looked everywhere – on the floor... beneath the chairs... under the cushions.
The ring wasn't there.

In the hall... in the cupboard...

and inside Catriona's coat pockets and gloves.
The ring had vanished.

Catriona sat at the foot of the stairs, feeling worried.

Then Mac thought of one place they hadn't looked...

Mac crouched on his tummy and gazed up at the tree, his whiskers twitching. There, near the top, was the tiny wink of light. "It's my star," he thought.

He leapt onto the trunk and clambered higher and higher. The tree began to dip and sway. At last he grasped the star between his teeth. TUG! But the tug was too much for the tree, which slowly toppled over... and with an ear-splitting...

CRASH

fell to the ground.
Tinsel and baubles went flying.

Catriona rushed in. "Mac! No! Our beautiful tree... Mum!"
Mac crawled forward to Catriona and opened his mouth.
Out rolled the star. Only it wasn't a star...

"The ring! It must have slipped off my hand when we pulled the tree through the window! Oh Mac..."

Catriona burst into tears. She had her ring back, but Christmas was ruined!

Mum stood in the doorway.

"Mum," Catriona sobbed. "Christmas is going wrong! First I lost my present and then Mac wrecked our tree."

"Now, now," soothed Mum, "I'm sure we can fix things. Suppose you tell me what's been going on."

Catriona put her head on Mum's shoulder and told her the whole story.

"...And I will never, ever, *ever* look at presents before Christmas Day again," she finished.

"I know you won't," agreed Mum, "and I don't think it will take long to clear up Mac's sparkly mess and make the house feel Christmassy again. Now, run upstairs and put that ring back. It won't be a surprise tomorrow, but that can be our secret."

"Only Mac knows," said Catriona, giving him a scratch on the head, "and he won't tell."

That evening, as they all sat down for tea, everything was ready for Christmas Day.

The last shopping had been done,

the last parcel wrapped,

and the Much Decorated Tree was more or less back upright,

so all the family went to the Christmas carol service.

Mac prowled around the silent house and kept watch over everything.

Late in the night, when Catriona was fast asleep, Mac looked out beyond the garden, the rooftops and into the sky. There he saw a wink of light. It was a star, mysterious and wonderful – a bright and shining Christmas star.